Miss Plunkett
to the
Rescue

Miss Plunkett to the RESCUE

by **Jane Flory**

Illustrated by **Blanche Sims**

Houghton Mifflin Company   Boston   1983

Library of Congress Cataloging in Publication Data

Flory, Jane, 1917-
  Miss Plunkett to the rescue.

  Summary: A former third-grade teacher comes out of
retirement to offer her services as a spy and risks her
life to save her country.
  [1. Mystery and detective stories. 2. Spies—Fiction]
I. Sims, Blanche, ill. II. Title.
PZ7.F665Mf 1983   [Fic]   82-15797
ISBN 0-395-33072-6

Printed in the United States of America

V 10 9 8 7 6 5 4 3 2 1

Contents

Miss Plunkett
to the
Rescue

1·Calling Miss Augusta Plunkett

*I*nspector General Frederick J. Ponsonby looked around Miss Plunkett's little parlor. It was just what he had expected of his former third-grade teacher. Family portraits on the wall, a well-used dictionary, the old class photographs with all the students lined up and smiling. There he was in one of them, in the middle of the back row. There was a Certificate of Merit presented by the School Board when Miss Plunkett retired. And everywhere the framed mottoes.

" 'A place for everything and everything in its place,' " he said. That was one of Miss Plunkett's favorite sayings.

She nodded approvingly, and passed the muffin plate again. "I'm glad you remember. You were not, as I recall, my neatest student."

He blushed. Freddy Ponsonby had been a small pear-shaped boy, spotted and untidy. Now he was a large pear-shaped man, and not much neater.

When she had finished her tea, Miss Augusta Plunkett set down her cup. "Now Freddy, tell me what is on your mind. I feel sure you are here for more than a social call."

He sighed. Nothing had changed. Miss Plunkett had always been able to see right through him.

Miss Plunkett even looked the same. She was still small and thin and straight as a ramrod. Her eyes were as bright as ever, as quick to show her impatience with stupidity. Be fair, he reminded himself. Miss Plunkett had always been generous with praise for anyone who really tried. No, nothing had changed. She was exactly the same, which is the reason he was here.

"Miss Plunkett," he began in a most solemn voice.

"Your coat sleeve is dragging in the jelly, Freddy."

Embarrassed, Inspector General Frederick J. Ponsonby started to lick the jelly from his sleeve. Just in time, he reached for his handkerchief. He wished he could have worn his uniform on this top-secret visit. Even Miss Plunkett would be impressed with all that gold braid.

He began again. "I don't have to tell you the most important manufactured product of Pugwell — "

"Noodles," she said. "Five hundred thirty-three million, four hundred twenty-seven and one half tons of noodles a year. Our country is the world's leader in noodle production."

"Until now, Miss Plunkett. But a truly terrible thing has happened, and we need your help. Until now, only we Pugwellians possessed the secret, the great Dandy Doodle Noodle Machine."

"And now?"

He leaned toward her and whispered.

"The plans of the Dandy Doodle have been stolen!"

"Stolen?"

"They must be recovered at all costs, or Pugwell will lose its worldwide noodle leadership. For this mission we need someone with a keen logical mind, a gift for making quick decisions, someone who does not know the meaning of fear. You, of all people, fit that description."

Miss Plunkett nodded. "Yes, I must say I do," she said.

"Also, you are unknown to the enemy. That is even more important."

She sniffed. "It is just possible that they may have heard of me, Freddy. After all, my reputation as a teacher may have spread."

"Miss Plunkett, will you do it? Will you accept this dangerous assignment? For it is indeed dangerous. International spies are involved."

Miss Plunkett fixed her bright eyes upon him. He tried to sit up straighter and pull in his stomach.

"You never were a good student, Freddy. In fact, you were one of my denser pupils. How you have risen so high in our country's service I cannot imagine."

3

"Yes, Miss Plunkett," said the great Inspector General meekly.

"However, as I recall, you had one good quality. Little Freddy Ponsonby was absolutely truthful. It is for this reason that I choose to believe your far-fetched story. I will think it over and let you know."

"There is no time to waste, Miss Plunkett. We have good reason to believe that the plans are already in the city of Piltweg, near the border. And we think they will soon be taken out of the country. If you decide to accept this assignment, you will have to leave tonight."

"So soon?"

"Not a minute later. Our country's Gross National Product is in grave danger."

"Then of course I must say yes."

"Then come to the Bureau tonight and we will give you a thorough briefing."

"I'll be packed and ready to go," she promised. "I will make any sacrifice in the service of my dear country."

He gave a sigh of relief and reached for another muffin. She frowned.

" 'Waste not, want not,' you always taught us," he reminded her with his mouth full.

"If you will recall, I also taught, 'Let not your eyes be bigger than your stomach,' " she said severely.

The Inspector General sighed again and tugged at his waistcoat. It was not easy dealing with Miss Augusta Plunkett.

2 · Into the Darkness Alone

*I*t was about midnight when Miss Plunkett arrived at the Bureau of International Prying and Spying. The huge door opened a crack at her knock.

"Give the password," whispered a hoarse voice.

" 'Whatever is worth doing is worth doing well,' " she whispered back. The door swung open. The Inspector General himself quickly drew her aside and locked the door behind her.

"What is all this nonsense, Freddy? You know perfectly well who I am."

"In our business we can't be too careful."

He led the way down one winding corridor after another. From time to time, their way was barred by a heavy door that he opened with a master key chained to his wrist. Lights flashed red and then green, and they passed through. He hoped Miss Plunkett was impressed.

"Here we are," the Inspector General said as they came at last to his office.

Miss Plunkett looked around at the heavy draperies, the thick carpet, the immense desk covered with documents, and nodded.

"You've done well for yourself, Freddy. This is quite comfortable. But do take off that ridiculous jacket. All that gold braid is making you round-shouldered."

Inspector General Frederick J. Ponsonby sighed. "Please sit down, Miss Plunkett. Before you leave we must explain exactly what you will be required to do."

He rang a bell on his desk, and his young assistant came bounding into the room.

"This is the Under-Deputy in charge of Overseas Meddling, P. Williamson Peters."

"Welcome aboard, Miss Plunkett," Peters said cheerily. "Since we're to work together, just call me Pete, and I will call you Gussie."

The Inspector General winced. The roses on Miss Plunkett's hat quivered. Miss Plunkett looked at Mr. Peters, and the Under-Deputy shivered as if he had felt the wind off an iceberg.

"Miss Plunkett will do fine, Mr. Peters," she said. "Now I suggest we get on with our business. We have frittered away quite enough time as it is." She looked sternly at the Inspector General, and he found himself squirming in his chair just as he had done so long ago in Miss Plunkett's third-grade class.

"As I told you, someone has stolen the secret plans of the Dandy Doodle Noodle Machine," the Inspector General said. "We think the culprit may be a scoundrel named Fast Eddy. We have traced Eddy to the Hotel Metropole in Piltweg, and we suspect he is even now offering the plans to the highest bidder. And if he is, the highest bidder will certainly be our enemy, Nether Dilchwood."

He paused to let this terrible news sink in.

"If the plans reach Nether Dilchwood, there is no hope, no hope at all."

Miss Plunkett blinked. She swallowed hard. *Nether Dilchwood.* The very words sent a chill down her back.

Where Pugwell was a country of gentle hills and pleasant valleys, Nether Dilchwood was all steep mountains, poor stony land, and people who were as sharp and treacherous as the storms that tore through the mountain passes.

She swallowed again and then asked bravely, "What will my duties be?"

"You must get the plans from Fast Eddy and bring them safely to us. It will not be easy. I would go myself if I were not so well-known in the spy community. Our reports tell us that Dirty Digby, the master spy of Nether Dilchwood, is starting this very minute for Piltweg, our capital city. His only purpose must be to buy those plans from Fast Eddy. You must get there first."

She nodded.

"We have no picture of Digby, no description even.

We know only that he is perhaps the trickiest spy in the entire world. Avoid him at all costs. For all we know he may be aware of our intention to send you. The Secret Service of Nether Dilchwood is extremely clever."

"I see that I must use my keen logical mind to outwit this Dirty Digby. I will start at once."

"This is an extremely dangerous expedition," the Inspector General warned. "Don't call attention to yourself in any way. Be inconspicuous. Get the papers and come right back. Whatever happens, *do not go into Nether Dilchwood!* No spy ever returns from there, *ever!*"

With a serious look he handed her the tickets and a map of Piltweg. She tucked them into her large handbag and stood up.

"Good-bye for now, gentlemen."

"Good-bye, Miss Plunkett, and — courage. Be brave."

"That goes without saying," she said.

Inspector General Frederick J. Ponsonby watched Miss Plunkett disappear into the night.

"I cannot do it, Peters! I cannot let Miss Plunkett go alone into this danger. Take over here. Keep things running until I get back."

He grabbed up the spy bag that he kept always packed and ready.

"I won't let her out of my sight. No harm must come to that remarkable lady."

3·The
Enemy Agent

*M*iss Plunkett was too excited to go to sleep, although the bus was not due at Piltweg until early morning. She opened her handbag and unfolded the map the Inspector General had given her.

To Miss Plunkett's disappointment, they had decided that her best disguise was no disguise at all. She was traveling as a retired third-grade schoolteacher. She would have preferred something more dramatic, and indeed had come prepared. She had stopped at a Spy Store on her way to Freddy's office. Her large handbag contained a change of costume, just in case.

"No, no disguise," said the Inspector General. "This way, if you are lost or confused no one will pay any attention. All tourists are lost and confused."

She sniffed. "I've never been lost or confused in my

life, but if it is necessary, I trust I can give a convincing imitation."

So now she settled back in her seat like an ordinary tourist. She spread out her Piltweg map and pretended to locate the cathedral.

When she was sure she knew exactly how to get to her hotel, the Metropole, she put the map away. She sat quietly, looking out at the black night.

She could see nothing outside, only the reflections of her fellow travelers, most of them asleep by now. A portly businessman was dozing over his snack, a well-dressed couple snored loudly. Only one other passenger was awake, reading his newspaper.

She leaned back and closed her eyes. Then she opened them a very little, and looked again at the reflection in the window. She had been right the first time. The one wide-awake passenger was holding a newspaper, but he wasn't reading it. Over the edge of his paper he was looking directly at her.

An Enemy Agent!

She held tight to her handbag and pretended to be asleep. The bus rocked along, up and down hills and valleys.

Twice she got up and changed her seat, and twice the newspaper reader changed his seat, too. She could feel his sharp gaze boring right into the back of her head, and she wondered if he could read her thoughts.

The sky was getting lighter. There was a beautiful sunrise, but Miss Plunkett hardly noticed. She was too busy making a plan.

She changed her seat again, just as the bus swerved around a corner. The Enemy Agent, following her down the aisle, let his paper slip and she got a quick look at him.

Tallish, paunchy, rather nice brown eyes, heavy eyebrows, big nose, glasses, bushy mustache — she memorized his appearance. "I'd recognize him if I saw him again." But she wanted to be sure she didn't see him again.

When the bus pulled in at the Piltweg station, Miss Plunkett took her time. She made sure the Enemy Agent was right behind her. As she reached the bus door, she suddenly lost her balance and lurched backward.

Pow! she hit the Agent in the stomach with her sharp elbow, and Wham! she stepped on his foot, grinding her heel into his big toe. Flap! her handbag swatted him across the face. For a moment, at least, he was out of business.

"Oh pardon me, sir," she said, and rushed from the bus, pushing her way through the crowds of travelers.

"Which way to the rest room?" she asked a porter.

A short time later a small bent figure peered out of the Ladies' Rest Room, adjusted her glasses, and wiped her large nose. She looked quickly around and picked up a push broom the porter had set aside. His back was turned as he emptied a trash can.

She was surprisingly agile for one who seemed so old and bent over. Before the porter had banged down the can she had swept her way across the room and out the door.

"I'll send him the money for the broom," Miss Plunkett thought as she swept up the peanut shells and candy wrappers in the square. "I'd hate to have it taken out of the poor fellow's salary."

If her memory was right, and it usually was, the Hotel Metropole was just down the street and around the corner. Before she rounded the corner, she stood the broom against a street lamp and whipped off her disguise. Only then did she notice that the false nose had a bushy mustache attached to it.

"That may have been a mistake," she thought. "I may have attracted attention to myself."

But the Enemy Agent was nowhere in sight. At any rate it was too late to worry. She had arrived at the Hotel Metropole.

4 · Mayhem at the Metropole

The Inspector General had engaged a room for her at the Metropole. She was both hungry and sleepy, but this was not the time to think of herself. She would rest and eat on the way home, when she had the secret plans safely tucked in her handbag.

First, though, she had to get the plans.

According to the Inspector General's information, they were now in the hands of Fast Eddy, a dastardly schemer who was loyal to no country, who served anyone who paid him well. His room was down the hall from hers.

She studied the layout of the third floor of the Metropole. Here was her room, 304, overlooking a back courtyard. Here was the elevator, and next to that the linen closet. A few doors farther along was 311, fronting on the main street. If the Inspector General was right, Fast Eddy was there now, awaiting the arrival of agents from various interested nations. The secret plans of the Dandy Doodle Noodle Machine would go to the highest bidder.

" 'There's many a slip 'twixt cup and lip,' " Miss Plunkett said. "Fast Eddy, you may have met your match."

She opened the door and peered into the hallway. It was empty, except for a chambermaid who stood at the open door of the linen closet, piling clean towels on her cart.

Miss Plunkett watched as the maid opened Room 310 and went in. In a few moments she was out again with a bundle of mussed sheets and towels. She turned toward 311.

"Now!" said Miss Plunkett. She slipped out of her room, closed the door silently behind her, and sped down the thickly carpeted hall. The chambermaid's back was turned, and she was humming.

Miss Plunkett came up behind her. As she shoved, she grabbed the chambermaid's ring of keys. The surprised maid folded up neatly into the laundry cart and Miss Plunkett wheeled it swiftly into the linen closet.

The chambermaid's song turned into muffled cries for help.

"No need to carry on," said Miss Plunkett. "There's plenty of air," and she slammed the door.

"Now!"

With the keys in her hand, she turned to 311 and saw an elderly waiter limping down the hall toward her. He hesitated as he heard the chambermaid bumping and bellowing in the closet. Miss Plunkett acted quickly. Burdened with a breakfast tray and taken by surprise, he was no match for her.

She whisked open the closet door and put out her foot. As he stumbled, she pushed him, tray and toast and cream pitcher, into the closet.

"In you go. 'Don't cry over spilt milk,'" she added as the cream pitcher tipped. She slammed the door in his face and then locked it.

Her last glimpse of him was of a long beard, bushy mustache, big nose, and gentle brown eyes behind his glasses. There was something very familiar about those eyes, but Miss Plunkett had no time to wonder where she had seen them before.

Now, at last, the coast was clear. She tried one, two keys in the lock of Room 311. The third turned smoothly, and she stepped inside.

Someone else had gotten there first.

Room 311 had been ransacked.

Bureau drawers were overturned on the floor, a suitcase was open and its contents dumped. The closet door stood wide open. Someone had searched the room from top to bottom, and not very long ago, either.

A limp figure was stretched out on the bed.

"Fast Eddy!" she whispered, horrified. She had studied his picture in the Inspector General's office.

As she watched, his lower lip quivered and he moaned.

"He's had a quick one-two to the choppers," she diagnosed, much relieved. "He's out cold, but he won't be out long."

She had to move fast.

The plans were gone; she was sure of it. All she could do now was hope to find a clue to their whereabouts in the disordered room.

The window had been flung open and a breeze was blowing the curtains. In the ivy below the window, sparrows were chirping indignantly.

Someone had clambered down the ivy vine only a moment before. A stout fellow, she guessed, for the heavy old vine had been torn from the wall in places, and a sparrow's nest teetered dangerously.

A small piece of paper was caught in the ivy leaves below. Miss Plunkett hung out of the window and snatched it, just as an angry sparrow was about to tear it to shreds.

It was a train ticket, Piltweg to Nether Dilchwood.

Miss Plunkett shivered. Could the heavy person who had assaulted and robbed Fast Eddy be Dirty Digby, the cleverest spy of Nether Dilchwood? Were the plans of the Dandy Doodle Noodle Machine already in his hands?

"You are not all that clever, Dirty Digby," said Miss Plunkett grimly. "Augusta Plunkett is on your trail."

5 · Move Fast, Miss Plunkett

*F*ast Eddy moaned. His eyelids fluttered.

Gracious! She had to leave at once! She peered out the door and saw that already the shouts of the waiter and the chambermaid had drawn a crowd.

It was a terrible predicament, but Miss Plunkett hesitated only a moment. Out of her handbag she took her spy disguise. She adjusted the false nose and then remembered the mustache.

Fast Eddy's nail scissors were on the dresser, and working quickly, she trimmed off the black bush. Over her rose-covered hat she tied on a large old-fashioned sun bonnet. The cover on the bedside table would do for a shawl. She draped it over her shoulders and slipped out of the room.

She did not notice that Fast Eddy had opened his eyes and was staring straight at her.

The manager was struggling with the key to the linen closet, and the maids gathered around were urging him to hurry. In the confusion, she walked briskly by. No one noticed her at all.

Suddenly there was a burst of cheering as the linen closet door flew open. There was a mixture of voices shouting, "She pushed me! She's the one! Stop her!" Someone else cried, "Wait! Please wait for me!"

The waiter was limping down the hall after her. Behind him staggered Fast Eddy, shouting, "Stop thief! I've been robbed, and that old lady did it!"

She managed to slam her door and lock it. She flung open the window and skimmed down the fire escape into the courtyard below. For the moment she was safe.

Now for the railroad station and Dirty Digby.

She hurried out the alley and around the corner. As she passed the ivy-covered wall, she hesitated. If Dirty Digby had dropped his railroad ticket, perhaps he had dropped some other clues as well. Her sharp eyes saw several things.

A coin, a snapshot of two fat babies, a bubblegum wrapper. She could not be sure that any of this belonged to Dirty Digby, but they were worth thinking about later so she put them all into her handbag.

She made two more sharp turns and stopped several times to peer into shop windows. No one seemed to be following her, so she hurried across Market Square. In a short time she reached Piltweg's railroad station.

"Next train to Nether Dilchwood leaves in half an hour

on Track 9!" shouted the Station Master. "Have your tickets ready!"

Phew! She had a few minutes to catch her breath and decide what to do next.

"I'll sit at the lunch counter," she decided. She would have a clear view of the ticket window. With his ticket lost, Dirty Digby would have to stand in line for another. But what would she do after that?

"Cross that bridge when you come to it," she said. " 'Never trouble trouble until trouble troubles you.' "

A mother with five boisterous children was first in line. Then came a tall, thin, impatient fellow, then several very ordinary travelers. She watched these closely, but none seemed to be Dirty Digby. She had no idea what Dirty Digby looked like, but she was sure she could tell a spy when she saw one. She was certain none of these travelers were anything but what they seemed.

The waitress behind the lunch counter brought a pot of tea. Miss Plunkett never took her gaze from the ticket window.

The line thinned out and the passengers for Nether Dilchwood were gathering at Track 9. Would Dirty Digby never come? Had she perhaps been wrong?

"Never!" said Miss Plunkett firmly. "I have been slightly mistaken several times in my life, but I have never been entirely wrong. He will come."

The hands of the clock crept closer and closer to departure time, and still no one who looked at all like her idea of Dirty Digby had come.

"All aboard!" shouted the Station Master. "All aboard for Nether Dilchwood!"

Suddenly Miss Plunkett felt a chill of excitement. A stout mustachioed porter stepped up to the ticket window, bought a ticket, then took up his broom again, and went sweeping across the station toward Track 9. Why would a porter need a ticket?

"You can't fool me, Digby," said Miss Plunkett. "I've used that trick."

She had been pouring a cup of tea, and the pot was still in her hand. She slipped off the stool and hurried after the porter, forgetting to set down the pot.

"Stop," screeched the waitress. "Bring back that teapot! You haven't paid yet!"

The station door swung open and a group of people shoved inside. Miss Plunkett was astounded to see the waiter from the Metropole, waving his tray and shouting, "Wait, wait! Don't take that train!"

Behind him Fast Eddy shouted, "Stop her! Stop the thief!"

The chambermaid followed, yelling, "Stop her! She's the one!"

The whistle blew and the train began to move. The porter dropped his broom and leaped for the steps. He reached down and swung Miss Plunkett up just as the train

began to pull out. The teapot smashed as her feet flew off the ground.

"Gave them the slip, did you, old girl?" the porter asked. He laughed heartily. "Well, so did I!"

6 · Nether Dilchwood, Here We Come

*B*efore Miss Plunkett could catch her breath, she was shoved into a vacant seat.

"Here we go, old girl. They can't catch us now!"

In a few moments the train rounded a curve, and the Piltweg station was out of sight.

"Well!" The stout gentleman settled back in his seat. "This was a good day's work in every way. Got what I came for, didn't have to pay a penny for it, and got away clean. Timed it right on the button. Pretty smart, eh, old girl?"

Miss Plunkett answered, " 'Pride goeth before a fall.' "

"Not with me it doesn't, not with Dirty Digby — not with Digby Grigsby. No fall at all."

" 'There's many a slip 'twixt cup and lip,' " she said. "They could catch us yet."

"Not a chance. In exactly one hour we'll be over the

border into Nether Dilchwood. They won't dare follow us there."

Nether Dilchwood. She was on her way to Nether Dilchwood, from whence no spy ever returned. For a moment Miss Plunkett's courage failed her. Then she said to herself, "Somehow you must accomplish what you set out to do, Augusta Plunkett. 'Where there's a will there's a way.' "

The conductor collected the tickets. Dirty Digby settled back in his seat and yawned. He patted his coat pocket, and Miss Plunkett heard the crackle of paper. The plans, the plans of the Dandy Doodle Noodle Machine were right there in his pocket under his hand. She was sure of it.

How was she going to get hold of them?

First, she must try to get word to Freddy Ponsonby. If she never returned, at least the Inspector General must know that she had done her best.

She rummaged in her handbag for a pen and postcard.

She had to choose her words carefully. She must not make the message too plain in case the card fell into enemy hands.

"Slight change in plans. Traveling eastward with Unclean D. Risky, but 'Nothing ventured, nothing won.' Scenery spectacular. Wish you were here."

There was a space left at the bottom of the card. It seemed a shame to waste it so she added, " 'To make an omelet, you must first break an egg.' "

"A nice thought," she said, "and one of my favorite

mottoes. It will give Freddy something to remember me by."

Digby groaned and stirred, and she hastily wrote the address before he awakened. She realized that she had no stamp, and for just a second she panicked. Then she said to herself, "You were not a third-grade teacher for nothing, Augusta Plunkett. Use your head."

She reached under the seat, and sure enough, some third-grader had left a wad of chewing gum there.

"I might have known," she said. She stuck the gum to the card and pressed into it the coin she had picked up beneath the ivy vine. She hid the card under her shawl just as Dirty Digby woke up.

He grunted and stretched. "Stuffy in here. I need a breath of fresh air. Want to come along to the observation platform?"

Miss Plunkett didn't intend to let him out of her sight, so she followed him down the aisle to the end of the train.

"We'll soon be at the border." He smiled. "Back to Nether Dilchwood, my Home Sweet Home. Good-bye to Pugwell and good riddance. Although I must say I did a good piece of work there. I'm a clever one, I am."

He patted his pocket and chuckled. "I tell you, there's someone in for a big surprise when he wakes up, if he ever does."

Miss Plunkett shuddered. " 'Keep a stiff upper lip,' " she reminded herself. " 'It's always darkest before the dawn.' "

Things did look dark with Nether Dilchwood only minutes away. Miss Plunkett could see no way out of her dilemma.

"What's that?" asked Dirty Digby, leaning over the railing. "What's that coming along the track?"

Miss Plunkett peered, too. Whatever it was, it was coming along fast behind them. They watched as it came closer and closer. It was a handcar, operated by — gracious, it was the crowd from the station platform! There were the chambermaid and the waitress and, pumping away for dear life, Fast Eddy and the bearded waiter.

"Oh my!" gasped Miss Plunkett. "They'll catch us!"

Dirty Digby stared hard at the oncoming handcar. It was gaining fast.

"Only one of them is after me," he decided. "I don't know the others. You must be a very wicked old lady to have so many people after you," he added admiringly. "Well, we fooled them once; we'll fool them again. Come on, stick with me."

7 · Up and Away!

"**B**e ready to jump when I give the word, old girl. We're coming to a milk stop soon."

The train slowed, and as it rolled by the milk stop, a husky farmer heaved a milk can up to a man in one of the freight cars.

"Now!" said Digby, and they jumped. They landed heavily in a patch of brush beside the track.

"Keep your head down," hissed Digby.

Miss Plunkett couldn't have sat up if she tried, for the wind had been knocked out of her. She could hear the train roll away. A moment later the handcar went clattering past.

It was so close she could hear Fast Eddy and the waiter panting as they pumped, and the excited screams of the waitress.

Then there was silence. Digby poked his head up.

"They probably saw us jump," he guessed, "but they were going too fast to stop. Quick! Follow me!"

Her bonnet was knocked over her eyes and she couldn't see a thing. But she obeyed Dirty Digby. She intended to stick to him until she got the secret plans, no matter what. So she stumbled along behind him, over the rough ground.

"That farmer is still waving at the train," Digby chuckled. "This is our chance. Up you go."

Miss Plunkett straightened her bonnet and looked out. The farmer's tractor was standing there, and Digby evidently planned to use it.

"Up you go," he said again, and once more she obeyed. She scrambled up behind him on the tractor seat, he turned the switch, and they were off.

At the sound, the farmer spun around, but he was too late. Digby was off in a cloud of dust and already partway down the road.

They roared along, lurching and rolling and grinding. Dirty Digby shouted, "Never drove one of these before! How am I doing?"

She clung tighter to his waist and shouted back, "Faster, faster! He's still following!"

Dirty Digby swung off the road and zoomed across a field, the farmer following far behind.

At the second field the farmer gave up and turned back. Perhaps he had gone for help. She shouted this to Digby, but he didn't seem worried.

"Look up ahead!"

Through the dust she could see several large tents.

"We're in North County now, and that's the County Fair."

Miss Plunkett looked over her shoulder again. "They've left the handcar!" she squealed. "They're following by truck!"

"Where, where?"

Dirty Digby turned to look, and in that split second the tractor went out of control. It roared up a bank and into the fairgrounds. Dirty Digby swore a terrible Nether Dilchwoodian oath and jerked at the steering wheel. He was too late.

They rounded the corner and hit a tent pole.

Miss Plunkett couldn't be sure what happened next. She saw farmers trying to rescue the scattered fruits and vegetables. She closed her eyes tight and hung on while they crashed into a hot-dog stand and just missed a cotton candy stall.

Dirty Digby gunned the engine. There was a crash and a shower of paper.

"That was the ticket booth!" shouted Dirty Digby. "We're here! We made it!"

She opened her eyes. A great striped balloon billowed above her. It was almost ready to take off, with a line of eager riders waiting to climb into the basket.

"Out of our way!" roared Digby. "Make way!"

One fellow already had one leg over the side of the basket. "Go to the end of the line," he said.

"This is the end of the line for you!" Digby gave him a push.

"You, there," shouted the balloonist. "You can't do that! Wait your turn!"

Digby hopped into the basket, with Miss Plunkett close behind him. Whatever happened, she was not about to let him get away.

"Take off," Digby ordered the balloonist. "This is a hijacking. We mean business!"

Miss Augusta Plunkett closed her eyes again. She was party to a terrible crime, and she did not want to know about it.

The balloonist begged, "Don't hurt me, Mister. I'll do what you say."

He pulled on a cord that sent up a burst of flame from the burner. The flapping balloon filled out with heated air. Then he untied the ropes that held them down and the balloon began to rise.

"Nice work," said Digby. "You're a sensible fellow."

"You won't hijack me! Take the balloon and fly it yourself!"

The balloonist flung himself over the edge.

Miss Plunkett did not want to look, but she had to know. She held her breath as he tumbled through the air, and then let it out as she saw that he landed unhurt.

Digby was watching too.

"A fine pickle we're in, old girl. We'll just have to learn to fly this balloon ourselves."

8·*What Goes Up*

*M*iss Plunkett took stock of the situation. Things were not good. Here she was, aloft in a hijacked balloon with an enemy agent. They were sailing east at a good clip, toward Nether Dilchwood. Things looked very grim indeed.

"What can I do?" she asked herself. "I must let Freddy know that I really tried," she thought, and she let the postcard she had addressed to him slip over the side of the balloon. Perhaps someone would find it and mail it.

She tried to think of a comforting motto, but the only one that came to mind was "What goes up must come down." Not much comfort there, since neither she nor Dirty Digby knew how to bring the balloon down safely.

She would have enjoyed the journey under other circumstances. The sky was clear, with a few little cottony clouds here and there. The basket rocked gently. They made no sound to disturb the quiet of the farms and fields below. But she took no pleasure in the pleasant scene.

She had come so far and dared so much, and it was all for nothing. The plans of the Dandy Doodle Noodle Machine were as far out of her reach as ever. She stared out at the ground and wondered what would become of her.

The road below, she noticed, was no longer deserted. A dark speck appeared, trailing a cloud of dust. As it drew nearer she could see that it was the truck that had been following the tractor. It was coming very fast. Far behind it a van was speeding along.

"They are still on our trail," she reported to Digby.

"Never mind them. We'll soon be in Nether Dilchwood, and then they'll get their ears pinned back proper."

Nether Dilchwood. It was not only the cool breeze that made Miss Plunkett shiver. Terrible, horrible Nether Dilchwood. The wind was carrying them due east, closer and closer. She looked at the setting sun — but wait! The sun was no longer directly behind them. The wind had shifted!

A slight shift more, and the balloon would be well inside the boundaries of Pugwell.

Miss Augusta Plunkett's spirits began to rise. She said to herself, "Up to now, Augusta Plunkett, you have let Dirty Digby call the tune. It is time for you to take charge."

First she had to get hold of the secret plans.

"Use your logical mind, Augusta Plunkett." She did, and an idea began to form.

"Oh dear, oh dear," she quavered. "The wind has changed and we're headed back over Pugwell!"

Dirty Digby was seated on the floor of the basket, trying to decipher the balloonist's instruction book.

"What?" he shouted. "That can't be!"

She pointed to the setting sun with a shaking finger.

"I'm so afeared," she said. "If those fellows down there catch me with these papers in my handbag, it'll be all up with me." She added in a pathetic voice, "You're such a fine kind gentleman, Mr. Grigsby. Would you, could you, hold these papers for me, just until we get away from them again? Oh, please, please."

She rummaged in her handbag and held out a little bundle — her guide book and a few travel folders — all folded inside the map of Piltweg.

"I'd do the same for you if I could, for I'm that grateful, I am, and I've nowhere else to hide them, no, I don't."

She babbled on as she handed him the packet. He stowed it away in his coat pocket without even looking at what she handed him.

"Not a bad idea, old girl. You *can* do the same for me. Fast Eddy down there would be glad to get his greasy paws on these again."

He handed over his bundle, and she stuffed it carelessly into her handbag, crying and trembling all the time until he said crossly, "Enough of the blubbering, old girl. Shut up and let me figure how to get this blasted balloon turned around."

"I'll help," she said, still sniffling a little. "You read out of the book and I'll follow your instructions."

"It doesn't say a word about turning it around. Only how to bring it down."

"And how is that?" Miss Plunkett asked, trying not to seem too eager. "How will we bring it down once we're safely over Nether Dilchwood?"

"To bring it down, you pull handle C, that's the big one on your right, then turn handles D and E — no, no! Not yet, not yet!"

Miss Plunkett jerked on handle C. The balloon leaned over and tipped out some of its air. They started to lose altitude.

Dirty Digby was knocked off his feet.

"Stop it!" he shouted. "We want to go up! More hot air!"

He lunged for the knob that controlled the burner, but Miss Plunkett jerked again at handle C and the blast of hot air was spilled out.

The ground lurched up, very close now. She braced herself for the crash.

Bam! Crunch! Smash! The wicker basket hit the ground and bumped along behind the deflated balloon.

Miss Plunkett leaped clear. She had made it! She was safe.

She heard a screech of brakes. The truck that had been following them had caught up at last. Fast Eddy jumped out.

"I've caught you! Give me back those plans, old lady!"

The waiter cried, "At last! Are you all right?"

Before she could answer, a screaming siren split the air. The van roared up and stopped. Someone said, "Stop in the name of the law! Don't make a move, any of you. You are all under arrest!"

9·More
Surprises

"You'll have plenty of time to be sorry for what you've done," said the Sheriff as he shoved them all inside his van. "It's jail for all of you."

Miss Plunkett was wedged onto a narrow bench between the waiter and the chambermaid.

"Only doing our duty, we were, trying to catch up with *her,* and now *we're* the ones arrested for Defiance of the Law," cried the waitress.

"And for stealing a handcar and a truck, and for Reckless Driving Without Due Regard for the Safety of Others," shouted the Sheriff. "Don't forget that."

The Sheriff was extremely cheerful. He had never before arrested so many criminals all at one time. This had been a good day's work for him.

The waiter was nudging Miss Plunkett to get her attention. "Did you get the secret you-know-whats?" he whispered. Miss Plunkett's eyes opened wide. "Did you get the plans?"

Another Enemy Agent! He wasn't a waiter at all. She clutched her handbag and looked straight ahead. Across the aisle Dirty Digby was waving his handcuffs and pointing to her handbag. He too wanted to know if the papers were safe.

Well, let them worry. She had the plans in her handbag, and come what may, she was not going to give them up.

When they arrived at the jail, she said to herself, "Be alert. Take note of everything. Look for a way to escape."

But the dark stone building did not offer much hope. It looked neglected, forgotten, miles away from nowhere. Miss Plunkett got a glimpse of empty fields all around and a skyful of mountains brooding in the distance.

Inside, the jail was no better. Damp stone corridors, high barred windows. The Jailer's office was bare and uncomfortable, brightened only by a large cross-stitched motto hanging over the desk.

"Too Many Crooks Spoil the Broth," it said. Miss Plunkett did not smile.

"They'll have to be searched," said the Sheriff happily. "Concealed weapons."

"You don't have to tell me what to do," said the Jailer. "I know my job, I do." He bellowed, "Matron!" and when no one came he yelled, "Wife, get in here!"

A poor meek little thing scuttled in, wiping her hands on her apron.

46

"Search the females," the Jailer ordered.

The waitress and the chambermaid shook out their petticoats to prove they had no concealed weapons.

"Where would I get a weapon?" sobbed the chambermaid. "I didn't even bring a hanky."

Miss Plunkett handed over her spare handkerchief. It seemed the least she could do for the frightened creature, who was crying too hard to do more than tell her name. "Emma," she sobbed. "Em — Emma."

Lucy, the waitress, glared at them all as she patted Emma's back. "There's no justice here," she said. "My Congressman will hear about this."

The Sheriff and the Jailer searched Fast Eddy. Then they turned to Dirty Digby.

"Here's the one who stole the tractor and the balloon. You'll not do that again, you hairy scoundrel!"

The Sheriff gave Digby's mustache a nasty tug.

"I've pulled off his nose!" he gasped.

Nose, mustache, and glasses had come off in his hand.

"Dirty Digby?" asked the Enemy Agent in the waiter's suit.

"Who else?" said Miss Plunkett nonchalantly, trying not to look surprised at the false nose and mustache.

"They are a sneaky pack of rogues," roared the Sheriff. "Let's see what that one's hiding!" he pointed to Miss Plunkett.

"Unhand me!" said Miss Plunkett, so fiercely that the Jailer's wife shrank back behind her husband. "I'll attend to this myself."

She untied the bonnet that hid her rose-covered hat. Then she removed her false nose and glasses.

"I am none other than Miss Augusta Plunkett."

Dirty Digby gulped, "A faker!"

"No more than you, Dirty Digby. Digby Grigsby, ha!"

"I said they were sneaky," said the Sheriff. "Him next."

"I'll decide who's next," said the Jailer. He pushed the Sheriff aside. "Him next."

The only one left was the waiter. The Enemy Agent.

The Jailer tugged at the waiter's beard. He ripped off the mustache and nose and glasses.

"Not a real nose in the lot!"

This time Miss Plunkett could not conceal her surprise. The waiter, also the Enemy Agent from the bus, was Inspector General Frederick J. Ponsonby.

10 · Miss Augusta Plunkett, Jailbird

Dirty Digby bellowed with surprise and rage.
"Ponsonby! The Inspector General! And as for
you — " he turned on Miss Plunkett. "I thought you were
just an ordinary wicked old lady. I was helping you get
away!"

Emma the chambermaid started to cry again. "It's all so
mixed up," she sobbed. "I can't tell if I'm coming or
going."

"You're going, the whole sneaky lot of you," shouted
the Sheriff. "Behind bars is where you're going until we
sort this out. If you have anything to say, say it at your trial.
Take 'em away," he yelled at the Jailer.

"It's my jail. They're my prisoners now. I'll decide what
to do with them," the Jailer retorted. "Matron, take 'em
away."

Miss Plunkett sat in her cell. She looked at the stone walls, the bars on the window and door. Her heart was pounding and she felt quite faint. Miss Augusta Plunkett, a jailbird. She choked at the very idea.

She thought of Freddy Ponsonby. He was in jail, too, and all because he had tried to protect her. She had treated him very roughly on the bus and in the hotel. She had made one mistake after another, and now she was in jail. For the first time in her life, Miss Augusta Plunkett had failed.

In spite of herself she began to sniffle a little. She reached into her handbag for her handkerchief, and under her fingers she felt Dirty Digby's bundle of papers.

Somehow in the confusion of all those false noses, they had forgotten to search her belongings.

At least she had the plans. All was not lost.

" 'Every cloud has a silver lining.' " She was so comforted by this thought that she repeated it aloud.

In the cell next to her Dirty Digby snorted. But Freddy, on her left, stopped pacing back and forth and replied, " 'It's a long lane that has no turning.' "

" 'It's an ill wind that blows nobody good,' " Miss Plunkett said.

" 'He who laughs last, laughs best.' "

Feeling much better, they sat down to wait for their supper.

After a long time they heard the Jailer's wife shuffling

along the passageway. She dipped out a bowl of something that she thrust between the bars of each cell.

It was dreadful stuff. As Miss Plunkett tried to choke down the meal, she had an idea. "Aha, the light at the end of the tunnel!" she exclaimed.

"That's my lantern," said the Matron. "I have to take it when I go. Eat up now, or you'll have to eat your supper in the dark."

"You call this slop supper?" shouted Dirty Digby and Fast Eddy together.

"I can't get it down," said Lucy.

"Me neither," said Emma, and she began to cry again.

"I do the best I can," said the Matron. "All that peeling and slicing, and my feet killing me. Nobody in this jail for years, and then this bunch shows up. What am I supposed to do?"

"A sprig of parsley might dress this up," said Miss Plunkett. "Perhaps if the turnips were diced smaller — "

"My land!" cried the harassed Matron. "Don't you go making my job any harder. Parsley! I've no time for making things fancy, indeed I don't. Not a minute."

"Of course you don't," said Miss Plunkett. "What you need is a scullery maid. Tomorrow I'll be right there, working beside you, peeling and chopping and slicing and baking, and all you'll have to do is give orders."

"My Mister — "

"He'll be delighted, I guarantee it," said Miss Plunkett. "First thing tomorrow, then. Please call me early."

After the Matron left there was silence in the cells.

"What are you up to?" asked Dirty Digby. "Are you feathering your own nest?"

"It's your nest, too," she retorted. "Tomorrow's meals will be fit to eat if I have anything to do with it."

Just before she went to sleep she heard a whisper. "Your keen logical mind is working on a plan, isn't it, Miss Plunkett?" Freddy asked.

"I do have a little something in mind," she answered. "Remember, 'Nothing ventured, nothing gained.' We must be bold."

"I knew you would think of something."

"Trust me," she said. " 'One step at a time.' "

Cheering Freddy made her feel better too. She could hardly wait until morning to get started on the first step.

11 · The Scheme Unfolds

*M*iss Plunkett was a whirlwind in the greasy kitchen. She chopped, she sliced, she stirred, she diced. And she did it all gladly, for Miss Augusta Plunkett had a scheme.

The meals improved greatly, but that was not the main thing. Each morning as she was let out of her cell Miss Plunkett counted her steps. Three hundred seventy paces down the hall, a sharp right, one hundred thirty more to the kitchen door. Seventeen to the sink by the window, allow five more for the thick stone walls. Each evening she wrote the figures on the bubblegum wrapper she had picked up under the ivy vine.

Next she suggested to the Matron that new curtains for the parlor might be nice. And the Matron, who had never in her life had such willing help, agreed.

Night after night in her cell, Miss Plunkett sewed on the curtains. When Dirty Digby accused her of currying favor, she replied, " 'A stitch in time saves nine.' In this case there are only six of us to save. At least we have the Matron's lantern now, and that is something."

After the curtains were hung, Miss Plunkett could write down the exact measurements of the parlor.

Next she made an expedition into the Jailer's office with a tea tray, counting to herself as she went. The Jailer's little eyes shone at the sight of the apple muffins. He gobbled five of them, hot and buttery and delicious. He patted his spotty vest, well filled out with the good food Miss Plunkett had been cooking. He belched happily.

" 'The way to a man's heart is through his stomach,' " she thought. She said to him, "This is a remarkably well-run prison. I hope Headquarters appreciates your efforts."

He scowled. "Headquarters! I wrote 'em days ago that I had this pack of criminals here, waiting for trial, and what was I to do? Did they answer? They did not! Throw my letters into the trash, they do, and let me wait. You could sit here for years, you could, waiting for a trial."

Miss Plunkett shivered. Pulling herself together, she said, "I guess they'd sit up and take notice if you had a recreation room in this fine up-to-date place."

"A recreation room? For that crew of thieves? Let 'em sit in their cells and repent." He belched again.

Miss Plunkett passed him another muffin and tried once

more. "There's a pantry next to the kitchen that nobody uses. It would free my mind for better things, like more baking, if I knew the prisoners were having a bit of exercise while we are all awaiting trial."

"Never!" He thought for a while. "Free your mind, would it?"

The next day he sent word by his wife that there was a pantry next to the kitchen that nobody used, and the prisoners would have to clean it themselves, and how about some more muffins?

That night Miss Plunkett explained her scheme to the other prisoners.

"I have drawn a map of the prison," she said. "In the floor of that pantry is a trap door to an unused cellar. If we dig five hundred thirty-nine paces north and seventy paces northeast, then a sharp turn to the right, no left — gracious, this paper is crumpled — and fifty-five more to get beyond the office, we'll come up in an old neglected garden. We'll be free!"

"Dig!" said Fast Eddy. "That's a lot of work."

Miss Plunkett gave him one of her looks.

"All right, I'll dig," he said.

He did. They all did, except for Miss Plunkett. She was busier than ever in the kitchen. The Matron spent most of her time in the parlor, no longer dark and dreary but clean and bright and cheerful with the new curtains and sofa cushions Miss Plunkett had made.

All the cooking was now up to Miss Plunkett. She took plate after plate of muffins and cupcakes and cookies into the Jailer's office. Whenever he was thinking he ought to make a little inspection trip, she would pop in with a hot apple pudding or a cherry cobbler. So he stayed at his desk and ate and wrote letters to Headquarters and waited for an answer.

Miss Plunkett found an old pack of cards, and three of the prisoners played noisy card games while two others were down in the cellar digging. Miss Plunkett stayed busy in the kitchen as a lookout.

The digging was hard work, but it was better than sitting alone in a dark cell. They had only their hands and bent spoons for tools, but they managed. When they were tired and discouraged Miss Plunkett cheered them.

" 'Slow and steady wins the race.' "

Sometimes Miss Plunkett's courage failed her. Sometimes in her cell at night she wondered if she would ever see her own dear parlor again.

Then Freddy would whisper, "We're doing fine. Your plan is working."

"Of course it is working. I never doubted it for a moment."

She sounded surer than she felt.

12 · Push to Freedom!

Dirty Digby had not forgotten the secret plans for the Dandy Doodle Noodle Machine. And Fast Eddy was sure Miss Plunkett was the thief who had knocked him out and stolen the plans. As the day of freedom grew closer, each one hinted that he intended to get the plans back.

But Miss Plunkett was just as determined as they. She had sewed the papers into the lining of her hat, and she wore her hat at all times, even when she slept. For now at least, the secret plans were safe.

Each day the tunnel grew a little longer. Each day their hopes grew stronger. Fast Eddy and Dirty Digby complained constantly, but they did their fair share of the digging and the card-playing.

"I never want to play another game of Fish again," said

Digby. "I'm so sick of Fish and War and Old Maid — "

"Hush your fuss," said Lucy, slapping down a king and winning the game.

"Shut up and deal," said Fast Eddy, and the card games went on, noisier than ever.

The noise gave the Jailer a comfortable feeling that all was well. It also drowned out the sound of scraping spoons in the cellar below.

Tired as they were, at night the prisoners talked and chattered in the darkness. Miss Plunkett was pleased at their commotion.

"The morale of the troops is high," she said. "I believe that to be a good sign."

Even Emma was cheerful. She no longer cried herself to sleep each night, and by day she did more than her share of digging.

At last Freddy, who had been put in charge of the tunneling, made an important announcement. "We are outside the wall," he said. "A short upward turn to the surface, and we're out and away!"

Fast Eddy was for finishing up and leaving at once. Emma and Lucy were ready to go, too. But Freddy and Dirty Digby sided with Miss Plunkett.

"If we rush it, we wreck it," said Digby. "I say we do this right."

"If we get caught now, we'll go into solitary confinement," Freddy said. "Quiet, please, everybody. Listen to Miss Plunkett's plan."

"I'm not gonna hang around this dump a minute longer than I have to," grumbled Fast Eddy.

"Not a minute longer," Miss Plunkett promised. "But if tomorrow I cook up a magnificent lunch, our captors will be lulled into a false sense of security. Perhaps they will be so stuffed they will even take a nap. That's when we can slip away."

"Sounds all right to me," said Lucy. The others agreed and Fast Eddy was voted down.

It was a long night. Miss Plunkett tried to calm them so they could all get the rest they needed. " 'All things come to him who waits,' " she called out.

" 'Early to bed and early to rise, makes a man healthy, wealthy, and wise,' " added Freddy.

"Above all, 'Here today and gone tomorrow'!"

With that last word from their leader, the little group settled down and went to sleep.

The next day went just as Miss Plunkett had planned. The card game was noisier than ever, and under cover of all the shouting, the last bit of digging went on.

"Only a few inches now," said Freddy. "We've struck something hard, a paving stone or some such. We'll give it a heave when we're ready to skip."

Miss Plunkett selected the menu carefully. She decided to serve luncheon in the parlor.

"What's this?" asked the Matron, as Miss Plunkett set the table.

"The office window overlooks the garden, that's what," thought Miss Plunkett. But she said, "It's a rather special luncheon. I knew you'd prefer it in here."

"I would?" asked the Matron.

"It's the latest thing," Miss Plunkett assured her. "All the best people have lunch in the parlor."

Miss Plunkett outdid herself that day, and when lunchtime came, she could hardly stagger under the tray she had prepared.

She made sure the Jailer and his wife had everything they needed. Then she hurried to join the rest of them in the cellar.

"The coast is clear," she reported. "Forward march! On to freedom!"

They crept down the long tunnel, hardly daring to breathe. When they reached the last obstacle, Miss Plunkett whispered, "All together now, heave!"

They heaved. The paving stone gave way. There was a mighty clatter, a light in the darkness, and — a screech from the Matron.

"The table is moving!" she screamed. "The soup has spilled!"

13 · All Is Lost

*T*hey had come up in the parlor.

    With one wrenching shove, they had heaved up a flagstone in the parlor floor, upset the table, spilled the lunch.

They crouched there in the tunnel looking up at the astonished faces of the Jailer and his wife, at the soup puddling around the chair legs, at the omelet on the floor, and at the apple muffins rolling away into the corners of the room.

For a moment or two they could not believe what had happened.

The Jailer also was too surprised to move. But only for a moment. Then his astounded yelp turned to a bellow of rage. It was all too horrible.

The Jailer herded them back to the cells, but not adjoining cells this time.

"There, you're all spread out. You won't catch me napping twice in a row, you won't."

Miss Plunkett was sunk in deep despair. She sat on her cot and tried to think where she had made the mistake. A few feet here, a wrong turn there. How could she, Augusta Plunkett, have been so mistaken? Augusta Plunkett, who had never been wrong in her entire life? She was responsible for this disaster. She had brought this down on the other prisoners' heads.

Finally she roused herself and tried to bring some cheer into the cheerless cell block.

" 'Where there's life there's hope,' " she said.

Dirty Digby jeered, "How about 'A penny saved is a penny earned'?"

"Yes," said Lucy. " 'A rolling stone gathers no moss.' Or 'Happy the bride the sun shines on.' "

Freddy remained loyal. " 'We see the stars clearest from the bottom of the well.' "

"Yeah, but who put us in the bottom of the well?" asked Fast Eddy. "Her, that's who. Miss High-and-Mighty, Miss Never-Been-Wrong, that's who."

Emma stopped sobbing.

" 'Onward and upward,' " she said pitifully.

It was only a small bit of support, but it comforted Miss Plunkett a little. "Thank you, Freddy and Emma," she said.

Then they sat there, silent in their cells. It was a long

discouraging afternoon and evening. Supper, when it finally came, was dreadful. Miss Plunkett could not eat a thing, and she set the greasy bowl aside.

"You should ought to eat something," said Emma suddenly from her cell across the way. "To keep up your strength."

"For what purpose?" asked Miss Plunkett bitterly.

"To get us out of here, of course," Emma said. " 'If at first you don't succeed, try, try again.' "

Miss Plunkett was amazed. "Someone still believes in me. In spite of everything, Emma believes in me, and I think perhaps Freddy does too."

"I must put my keen logical mind to work," she thought.

She sat up, put her rose-covered hat on straight, and began to think. But her thoughts were jumbled, full of regret that she had ever left her neat comfortable home, sad that she was now no more than a common jailbird in a dark untidy cell.

"Well, I can change some of that," she said determinedly. "I can clean my cell. After all, 'Cleanliness is next to godliness.' "

She made a makeshift broom of straw and batted away at the cobwebs. She turned her mattress and pounded the lumpy pillow. She hung up her water pail and washbasin. She climbed to the one narrow little window and scoured away a clear place on the dusty glass. At least she could look out.

What she saw gave her no cause for cheer. There was

only a range of high hills to the east of the prison. "The Dark Hills," she thought. Her heart sank. "The Dark Hills form the boundary of Nether Dilchwood." There was no help in that direction. No help at all.

Or was there? If Dirty Digby was Nether Dilchwood's top spy, would not his countrymen come to his rescue if they knew he was imprisoned? How could she let them know where he was? Suddenly she thought she knew.

She dumped her handbag out on the cot and scrabbled through the contents — comb, mirror, her house keys, the false nose she had been so pleased to purchase at the Spy Store, a snapshot of two fat babies — now where had that come from?

Then she remembered. She had picked it up at the foot of the ivy vine at the Hotel Metropole, along with a coin, a bubblegum wrapper — ah, here it was, her pocket flashlight. Miracle of miracles, the battery was still alive.

Then she called, "Digby? Dirty Digby? I have an idea."

Somewhere down the line of cells she heard Digby stir.

"Don't tell me about it," he said. "I don't want to hear any more of your great ideas."

She ignored that. "If you were to be rescued, would you promise to take all the rest of us, too?"

"I don't want to hear another word from you. Not now, not ever."

She heard the straw mattress rustle as Digby turned his back on her.

Was this to be the end of her new plan?

14·One More Try

"Listen to me, Digby. There is hope, there really is. Just tell me your spy code name."

"Never!" he shouted. "No good spy ever tells his code name!"

She heard the Matron shuffling along the hall, so she hurried back to her cot. She swept her few belongings into her handbag, and as she did, the snapshot fell to the floor face down. On the back was written, "Love from Valery and Jasper to Grandpa D."

Her heart raced. Perhaps Grandpa D was someone else, but she had to take a chance. When the Matron had gone she tried again.

"Please tell me your code name, Digby."

"Never!"

"Not even to be free to see your little Valery again? Not even to play with your little Jasper?"

She could hear him leap up and shake the cell bars. "How do you know about Valery and Jasper?"

Miss Plunkett smiled in the dark. "A good spy finds out everything. Trust me, Digby, and you'll be free to see your little grandchildren again. Now tell me your code name."

His voice fell to a hoarse whisper. "Never!"

"Never is a long time, Digby. Grandchildren grow up fast."

There was a long, long pause.

"I give up. It's 'Grandpa 299,' " he croaked at last.

"Never fear, Digby, I will use the information to help you, to help all of us," Miss Plunkett promised. "Trust me. I'll get us out of here."

In spite of themselves the other prisoners were hopeful and excited. "How?" they asked. "How soon?"

"Trust me," said Miss Plunkett grandly, and she climbed to the windowsill with her flashlight. "I will bring help to rescue us."

"Hooray!" they all cheered. "Three cheers for our Miss Plunkett!"

Then there was a long silence. Finally Freddy asked, "What's happening? Are you getting an answer, Miss Plunkett?"

"I just realized," she admitted in a very small voice. "I don't know Morse Code."

Digby let out a moan, and Fast Eddy jeered, "She's done it again. Miss Know-It-All's done it again!"

There was a chorus of hoots and catcalls. Miss Plunkett could hardly bear the humiliation.

Then Emma spoke up. "Morse Code is them dots and dashes, isn't it? Well, I remember them."

"You?" asked Miss Plunkett.

"I was a Girl Scout once," said Emma modestly. "Had to learn 'em to get my badge."

With Emma's guidance, Miss Plunkett was able to flash "SOS Grandpa 299" over and over. After each message she turned off her light and peered into the darkness. There was no answering flash from the Dark Hills.

Over and over, over and over, until her little light flickered and went out.

It was almost dawn. The battery was dead, and there was nothing more Miss Plunkett could do. She took off her rose-covered hat, lay down on her hard cot, and fell into an exhausted sleep.

15·What Now?

*S*everal hours later — Crash! Bang! Boom!
The whole jail rocked.

Clang! Whoosh! Smash!

Miss Plunkett was flung right out of bed. As the dust settled she heard voices calling, "Grandpa 299, come in 299. Where are you?"

"Here!" Miss Plunkett called. She scrambled to her feet. "Here! Remember, Digby, we all go together. 'All for one and one for all'!"

There was a huge hole where the front door had been. Three masked strangers were bending over the Jailer. They had tied his arms and legs and were taking the key ring from his belt. Without a doubt, they were Nether Dilchwoodians.

"This way," she called. "We're expecting you."

The rest of the prisoners were still dazed from the blast.

They wobbled to their cell doors, trying to figure out what had happened.

"Be of good cheer," she shouted. "Digby's countrymen have come to our rescue."

The three Dilchwoodians trotted down the hall, jingling the keys.

"Here we are, 299. We'll have you out in a flash."

"All of us," said Miss Plunkett.

"Sorry, ma'am, there's no room in the 'copter. Our orders say 'Grandpa 299' and that's all."

"Digby," said Miss Plunkett, "you promised."

"I never!" said Digby. "I never really promised."

"If you didn't you should have."

"Out of our way, ma'am. We haven't much time."

Miss Plunkett moved fast. She reached through the bars and grabbed the keys from the surprised rescuer. She flung them into the far corner of her cell.

"There," she said. "No one goes unless we all go."

The prisoners cheered, all except Dirty Digby. He looked at Miss Plunkett and she looked at him, straight in the eye.

Finally he gave in.

"She means it, fellows," he said to the rescuers. "Room or no room, we'll squeeze 'em in."

"But — "

"You heard 299," said Miss Plunkett. "Here are the keys. There's no time to waste."

76

As they passed the Jailer's office they all waved. The Jailer was writhing on the floor, trying to get free. The Matron sniffled and fumbled with the knots.

"Good-bye, good luck," called Miss Plunkett. "Remember, always dice the turnips fine. Use plenty of parsley, and a pinch of thyme never hurts — "

"No time, no time to waste," said the rescue team leader. "Let's get out of here."

As they stepped through the front wall, a procession of cars streaked up the drive. Sirens screamed, brakes screeched.

Miss Plunkett's heart sank like a stone. What now?

16 · Farewell to the Prison

The door of the first car flew open, and out stepped a familiar figure.

"Stop right there," he said to the rescue team, and the police surrounded the group. "Miss Plunkett, Inspector General, are you all right?"

It was Mr. Peters.

Dirty Digby groaned. "One more minute and we'd have been safely away."

"Sorry about that, Dirty Digby," said the Inspector General. "Looks as if your spying days are over. Handcuff him, officers, and Fast Eddy, too."

Dirty Digby turned pale.

Miss Plunkett thought of the leap from the moving train, the wild tractor ride, the balloon trip. It had all been wonderfully exciting. She owed Digby something.

"I will be a character witness at your trial," she promised. "You are wicked through and through, but you did help with the tunnel, and at the last you were as good as your word. You were going to help us all get away."

"Thanks for nothing," he snarled as they led him away. "But don't think this is the last of it. We Dilchwoodians will get our hands on the Dandy Doodle yet!"

"Don't hold your breath," advised Miss Plunkett.

"We have some loose ends to clear up," said Mr. Peters. "Let's go back inside."

They went in and untied the Jailer's bonds.

"I have some orders here from Headquarters," said Mr. Peters.

"At last," said the Jailer. "They've answered my letters."

"Not exactly. They expect to get an answer off to you someday soon. But right now, the prisoners are to be released as soon as we have settled a few bills." He opened his briefcase. "I'm not sure I understand all these items. We are to pay for — a wrecked tractor? A hot-dog stand, including hot dogs, rolls, and relish?"

"And mustard, too," said Miss Plunkett.

"A ticket booth?"

"And tickets."

"A stolen handcar? And a stolen truck?"

Freddy reddened.

"We agents do what we must, Peters," Miss Plunkett answered firmly.

"But this one — surely not a hijacked balloon?"

"It seemed necessary at the time, I assure you."

"Is that all?" asked the bewildered Mr. Peters.

"There's my bill at the Metropole. I'll return the hotel's table cover. I needed a shawl, you see."

Lucy reminded her, "Lunch at the station and the teapot. You ate and ran, you know. If I'd known what it was going to lead to, I'd have paid it myself and stayed home."

Mr. Peters wrote all this down, shaking his head.

"Anything else?"

Miss Plunkett. "Oh yes, a new broom for the porter in the bus station. I stole his."

He stared at her.

"I needed it to sweep up peanut shells, Mr. Peters."

"What about the front of my jail?" demanded the Jailer. "Not to mention the pain and distress."

Mr. Peters said, "You will have to bill Nether Dilchwood for that. Miss Plunkett had nothing to do with the explosion."

She cleared her throat.

"You didn't, did you? Miss Plunkett, *did* you?"

"In a manner of speaking. I signaled for the rescue team. But I never dreamed they would arrive with such a bang."

When they finally left Lucy and Emma in Piltweg, it was an emotional good-bye.

"I'll never forget this," said Lucy, shaking hands all around. "I wouldn't care to do it again, but I'll never forget it."

"Me neither," said Emma, awash in tears again. "Not so long as I live."

" 'Onward and upward,' Emma," said Miss Plunkett kindly, patting her on the back. "Remember, we have you to thank for the Morse Code."

Then she and Mr. Peters and Inspector General Frederick J. Ponsonby settled down in the limousine for the long ride home. She was just nodding off for a nap when she thought of something.

"How did you manage to track us down, Mr. Peters?"

"From the clue on your postcard."

"Clue?" She tried to remember.

"The secret code message at the end. 'To make an omelet you must first break an egg.' Aha, I said, one thing is clear. I will find her disguised as a cook somewhere. I had our men scour the countryside. We ate in every restaurant in Pugwell."

"Oh my," said Miss Plunkett faintly.

"It was difficult. Not every cook is a good cook, you know, but we kept at it. Many cases of heartburn later, when we had almost given up, I read the reports from a half-forgotten prison on the border. The Jailer mentioned apple muffins, and I knew at once what it meant."

"It was clever of you to send the message in such a secret code," said Freddy admiringly.

Miss Plunkett thought about it, and then decided it was not necessary to explain about the message.

"We agents have our methods," she said mysteriously.

"Success is what counts. The plans of the Dandy Doodle Noodle Machine are safe inside my hat. Let's just say, 'All's well that ends well.' "

Mr. Peters cleared his throat. "Ah," he said nervously. "The Dandy Doodle. Yes, indeed. Well, that brings me to the object of my trip. I hurried after you, Miss Plunkett, to let you know that — well, the truth is, the High Command has decided that Pugwell doesn't need the Dandy Doodle Noodle Machine."

"We don't need it?" gasped Miss Plunkett.

"I tried to find you before you went to too much trouble."

"Oh, it was no trouble," said Miss Plunkett bitterly. "Just no trouble at all."

Freddy could hardly believe it. "But Pugwell's Gross National Product is noodles, millions of tons of noodles. What do they plan as a substitute?"

"Apple muffins. Pugwell is going to be world famous for apple muffins."

Miss Plunkett settled back against the cushions and smiled. "Oh, of course in that case I don't mind all the trouble. Now my recipe is really very simple — "

Mr. Peters cleared his throat again. "Mrs. Snavely has offered her recipe. She — she's the wife of the Secretary of State."

That brought Miss Plunkett bolt upright.

"Mrs. Snavely's recipe? We'll have to see about that!"

Freddy hurried to change the subject. "One thing is certain, dear Miss Plunkett, your spying days are over. I will never allow you to be in such danger again. Never."

"Never is a long time, Freddy. We'll see about that, too."

"Yes, Miss Plunkett," he answered meekly.

Miss Augusta Plunkett was still in charge.

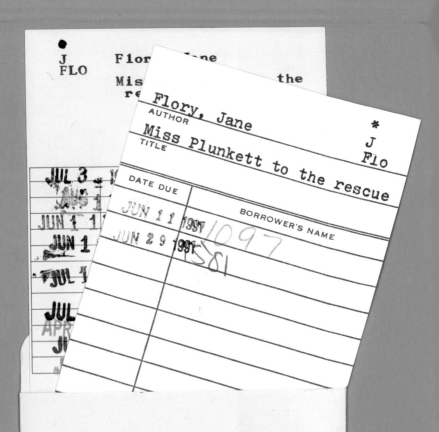